P9-ARB-468

HERE WE GO LOOBY LOO

Retold by STEVEN ANDERSON
Illustrated by TOM HEARD

CANTATA
LEARNING

WWW.CANTATALEARNING.COM

Washington County Public Library
205 Oak Hill Street
Abingdon, VA 24210

Published by Cantata Learning
1710 Roe Crest Drive
North Mankato, MN 56003
www.cantatalearning.com

Copyright © 2016 Cantata Learning

All rights reserved. No part of this publication may be reproduced
in any form without written permission from the publisher.

Library of Congress Control Number: 2015932807
Anderson, Steven.
Here We Go Looby Loo / retold by Steven Anderson; Illustrated by Tom Heard
Series: Sing-along Silly Songs
Audience: Ages: 3–8; Grades: PreK–3
Summary: Learn opposites in this fun dancing song.
ISBN: 978-1-63290-378-5 (library binding/CD)
ISBN: 978-1-63290-509-3 (paperback/CD)
ISBN: 978-1-63290-539-0 (paperback)
1. Stories in rhyme. 2. Opposities—fiction.

Book design, Tim Palin Creative
Editorial direction, Flat Sole Studio
Music direction, Elizabeth Draper
Music arranged and produced by Musical Youth Productions

Printed in the United States of America in North Mankato, Minnesota.
122015 0326CGS16

ACCESS THE MUSIC!
SCAN CODE WITH MOBILE APP
CANTATALEARNING.COM

Years ago in **England**, children sang "Here We Go Looby Loo" as they did a fun **dance**. This dance looked much like what we call the **Hokey Pokey** today.

So put on your dancing shoes and get ready to sing along!

Here we go looby loo.
Here we go looby lie.

Here we go looby loo,
all on a Saturday night.

Here we go way down low.

Here we go way up high.

Here we go way down low.

Oh, what a **wonderful** ride!

Here we go around fast.
Here we go around slow.

Here we go around fast.
Oh, what a great way to go!

Here we go up and down.

Here we sit side by side.

Here we go up and down.
We're having a wonderful time!

That was so much fun,
let's do it all again!

Here we go looby loo.
Here we go looby lie.

Here we go looby loo,
all on a Saturday night.

Here we go way down low.
Here we go way up high.

Here we go way down low.
Oh, what a wonderful ride!

Here we go around fast.
Here we go around slow.

Here we go around fast.

Oh, what a great way to go!

Here we go up and down.
Here we sit side by side.

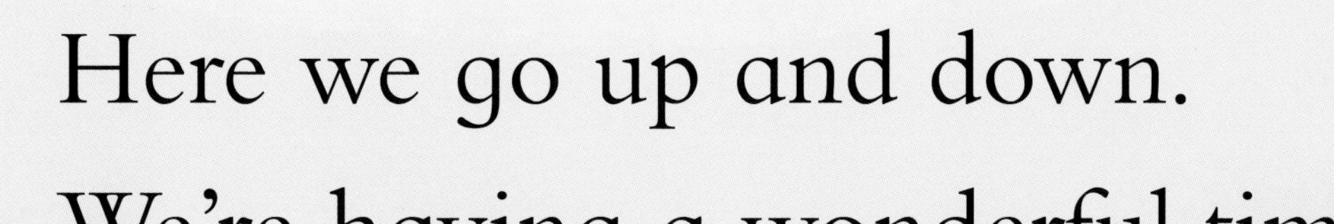

Here we go up and down.
We're having a wonderful time!

SONG LYRICS

Here We Go Looby Loo

Here we go looby loo.
Here we go looby lie.

Here we go looby loo,
all on a Saturday night.

Here we go way down low.
Here we go way up high.

Here we go way down low.
Oh, what a wonderful ride!

Here we go around fast.
Here we go around slow.

Here we go around fast.
Oh, what a great way to go!

Here we go up and down.
Here we sit side by side.

Here we go up and down.
We're having a wonderful time!

That was so much fun,
let's do it all again!

Here we go looby loo.
Here we go looby lie.

Here we go looby loo,
all on a Saturday night.

Here we go way down low.
Here we go way up high.

Here we go way down low.
Oh, what a wonderful ride!

Here we go around fast.
Here we go around slow.

Here we go around fast.
Oh, what a great way to go!

Here we go up and down.
Here we sit side by side.

Here we go up and down.
We're having a wonderful time!

Here We Go Looby Loo

Traditional Jazz/Dixieland
Musical Youth Productions

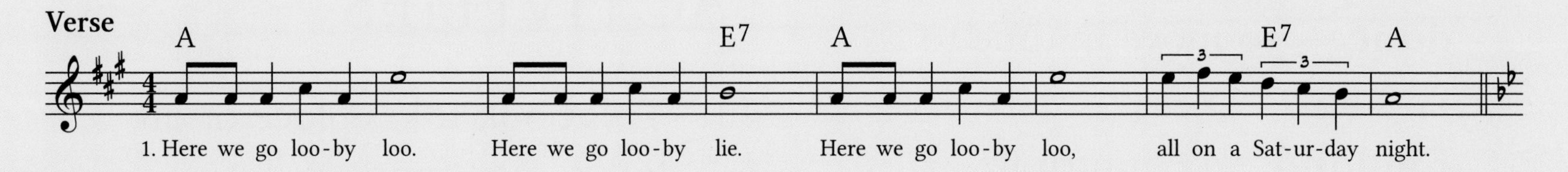

Verse 2
Here we go way down low.
Here we go way up high.
Here we go way down low.
Oh, what a wonderful ride!

Verse 3
Here we go around fast.
Here we go around slow.
Here we go around fast.
Oh, what a great way to go!

Verse 4
Here we go up and down.
Here we sit side by side.
Here we go up and down.
We're having a wonderful time!

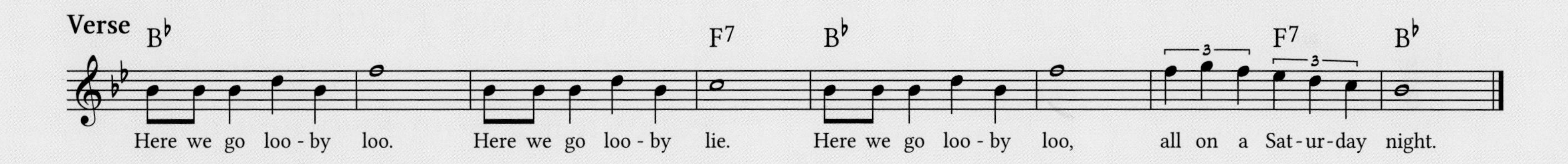

Verse 2
Here we go way down low.
Here we go way up high.
Here we go way down low.
Oh, what a wonderful ride!

Verse 3
Here we go around fast.
Here we go around slow.
Here we go around fast.
Oh, what a great way to go!

Verse 4
Here we go up and down.
Here we sit side by side.
Here we go up and down.
We're having a wonderful time!

GLOSSARY

dance—to move in time to music

England—a country in Europe

Hokey Pokey—a dance performed in time to a song and including several actions

wonderful—something that is very good or amazing

GUIDED READING ACTIVITIES

1. This book takes place at an amusement park. What is an amusement park? Have you ever been to one? What was your favorite thing to do there?
2. The children go "way up high" and "way down low." What ride does that? The children go "around fast" and "around slow." What ride does that?
3. Look on pages 14 and 15. These kids are getting treats to eat. What is your favorite treat? Can you draw it?

TO LEARN MORE

Feldman, Jean, and Holly Karapetkova. *Addition Pokey*. Vero Beach, FL: Rourke, 2010.

Freeman-Hines, Laura. *Here We Go Looby Loo: Children's Favorite Activity Songs*. Mankato, MN: Child's World, 2011.

Long, Ethan. *The Croaky Pokey*. New York: Holiday House, 2011.

Wood, Hannah. *Old McDonald Had a Farm: And Other Favorite Children's Songs*. Wilton, CT: Tiger Tales, 2012.